*Don't miss the other books in the series!*

# Real Kids Real Adventures™

## NUMBER

## DEBORAH MORRIS

BERKLEY JAM BOOKS, NEW YORK

REAL KIDS, REAL ADVENTURES #9:
EXPLOSION!

A Berkley Jam Book / published by arrangement with
the author

PRINTING HISTORY
Berkley Jam edition / September 1998

The Penguin Putnam Inc. World Wide Web site address is
http://www.penguinputnam.com

ISBN: 0-425-16429-2

**The Library of Congress has catalogued
the Real Kids, Real Adventures series as follows:**

Morris, Deborah, 1956–
Real kids real adventures / Deborah Morris.—Berkley ed.
        p.   cm.
    Originally published: Nashville, Tenn. : Broadman & Holman
Publishers, c1994–<c1995     >.
    Contents: 2. Over the edge ; Kidnapped! ; Swept underground—
3. Tornado! ; Hero on the Blanco River ; Bear attack!
    ISBN 0-425-15975-2 (pbk. : v. 2).—ISBN 0-425-16043-2 (pbk. : v. 3)
    1. Christian biography—United States—Juvenile literature.
2. Children—United States—Biography—Juvenile literature.
[1. Survival. 2. Adventure and adventurers. 3. Christian biography.]
I. Title.
[BR1714.M67   1997]                                              97-5391
277.3'082'0922—dc21                                              CIP
[B]                                                              AC

BERKLEY JAM BOOKS®
Berkley Jam Books are published by The Berkley Publishing Group,
a member of Penguin Putnam Inc.,
375 Hudson Street, New York, New York 10014.
BERKLEY JAM and its logo
are trademarks belonging to Berkley Publishing Corporation.

PRINTED IN THE UNITED STATES OF AMERICA

10   9   8   7   6   5   4   3   2   1

# Real Kids
# Real
# Adventures™

NUMBER

9

# Explosion!

## THE CHRISTOPHER WICE STORY

ABOVE:  Christopher Wice, practicing skateboard tricks.

"Hey, guys, check this out!"

Christopher Wice paused with one foot on his skateboard and waited for the others to glance in his direction. Most of them had been skating together for years on the streets of Barrie, a small city in southern Ontario. At age fourteen, Christopher was one of the oldest.

Several of his friends obediently stopped to watch.

"I'm gonna ollie down the stairs!" Christopher declared. They were in the parking lot behind the library, where they were sort of forbidden to skate. But skateboarding was serious business, and that sometimes meant taking risks.

Besides, with all the stairs, ledges, and curbs, there was no better location for miles around.

"Good luck," one boy scoffed. "You're gonna crash!"

Christopher shrugged, then pushed off with a

3

quick movement. His heart beat faster as he gathered speed. He tried to ignore all the eyes on him and focus on each movement. Skateboarding required incredible concentration.

*This is going to be good,* he thought as his front wheels reached the top of the concrete staircase. He dropped into a squat, kicked the tail of his board, and shifted his front foot—and suddenly, he was airborne! As the wind whisked through his short brown hair, he felt powerful, invincible.

Unfortunately, it was short-lived.

Abruptly, his balance shifted, his board slipped out from under him, and he hit the concrete. He went in one direction, his skateboard in another. The battered board sailed quite a distance before it clattered to a stop.

Crashing really stunk. It hurt, too. Christopher picked himself up as if it were no big deal. A couple of his friends smiled and shook their heads, but nobody laughed. They'd all kissed the pavement plenty of times.

Christopher stumbled over to pick up his skateboard, walking straight to conceal that his right knee was killing him. He looked at his board lying on its back, its worn-down wheels spinning in the air.

''I need a new skateboard,'' he muttered, snatching it up angrily. The problem was, how could he earn the hundred bucks or so he'd need to buy one?

The answer came sooner than he thought.

• • •

It was a sunny Saturday morning. Christopher usually slept in on weekends, but this time, when his alarm clock rudely jolted him from sleep, he jumped up with a smile. He was going to his grandparents' house for a week—one of his favorite places to go in the summertime.

His mother's parents lived in Thornhill, a quiet town outside Toronto. Whenever Christopher visited Nana and Papa, he had his own room and ate like a king; Nana loved to cook. Better yet, he could take the subway into Toronto for some serious skating.

This time, however, there was an added extra: his grandfather was going to pay him to help out around the house. He could use that money to buy the new Birdhouse skateboard he'd already picked out.

Pulling on his baggy jeans, sneakers, and T-shirt, Christopher quickly packed for the trip. Along with the usual clothes and stuff, he included a couple of his favorite skateboard videos. It helped to study how the pros skated.

He dropped his bag and backpack by the door and dashed out to the garage. "Dad!" he said. "When are we leaving?"

"A few hours," Steven Wice answered as he worked on his latest project.

Christopher watched as his father effortlessly assembled two pieces of pine using only one hand. Mr. Wice was born without a right hand, but he had never let it bother him. In fact, he was a talented artist who sold his work. He had a prosthetic (artificial) hand, but he rarely used it. He said it was more trouble than it was worth.

Christopher had learned many things from his father, like how to use different tools and how to repair things around the house. He'd be using those skills at his grandparents' house to earn his new skateboard.

"Why don't you have some breakfast before we go?" his father suggested. He didn't look up, so all Christopher saw was his thinning brown hair.

"Okay," Christopher said grumpily. After getting up early, he wasn't in the mood to hang around the house. He poked around in the refrigerator, but didn't see anything he wanted to eat. He decided to skip breakfast and wait for Nana's cooking.

His mom was doing her usual, dashing around the house and worrying that they were forgetting something. A short, fiery redhead with boundless energy, Colleen Wice often left the teenager feeling exhausted.

"Mum! Just calm down and come *on,*" Christopher said. "We're going to be here all day if you keep this up."

Mrs. Wice ran a hand through her hair. "Okay, then. But if you've left anything, you'll have to do without it for a week."

"Great. Let's go."

Once they finally left, the hour-and-a-half drive through Ontario's woods went by quickly enough.

If anything, it was monotonous. Christopher was half-asleep by the time his family pulled into his grandparents' driveway.

When the car stopped, he yawned and sat up. His grandparents lived in a gray two-story house with a large, glass-enclosed front porch and a two-car garage. But what really made it stand out was Nana's flowers. Colorful mums and impatiens were in full bloom, making bright spots of color against the gray brick.

As Christopher unbuckled his seat belt, his grandfather stepped out onto the porch and waved cheerfully.

"Come in, come in!" he called out in his rich Irish brogue. Christopher loved his grandfather's accent. It was a wonder it had stayed so firmly in place even though Papa and Nana had lived in Canada for many years.

Mrs. Wice trotted up the front steps and kissed her father's thin cheek. "Hi, Dad. How are you feeling?"

"Oh, about the same. I'm all right." Papa had serious heart and lung problems, but he didn't like to talk about it.

Mr. Wice was next in line. "I believe you ordered some hired help?" he joked, motioning toward Christopher.

Papa placed his hands solidly on Mr. Wice's shoulders. "Why, yessir, I did. Is this the best you could do?" His eyes shifted and he looked Christopher over, up and down.

"Ha, ha, very funny," Christopher said, his battered skateboard tucked safely under one arm. "Don't you worry. I'll deliver."

"I believe you will!" The old man swept Christopher and the skateboard up in a big hug. "You're going to help me paint the garage and work in your grandmother's garden, eh?" With his Irish accent, it came out sounding like, "garrr-age" and "garrr-den."

"Sure am," Christopher replied, his face muffled against his grandfather's flannel shirt. He was shocked at how skinny Papa felt. He had lost weight since the last time they'd visited. "I get to stay a whole week this time."

"Good, good. Now come on in and sit down. Your grandmother's got dinner cooking. She's even baked a big chocolate cake for dessert!"

Christopher's father grinned. "Mmmm, just what the doctor ordered."

Mrs. Wice cocked her head and tapped her husband's well-rounded stomach. "Oh, really? And which doctor was that?"

Christopher hid his smile as he bounded upstairs. His father loved chocolate cake, and his grandmother loved to bake. Good thing they didn't live any closer, or his father would weigh three hundred pounds!

Christopher tossed his bag and backpack into the upstairs closet, then propped his skateboard carefully against the wall. It might look bad, but it was his. Until he could afford a new one, he'd take good care of it.

He sat on the bed for a moment, then peeked out the window at the tree-lined street. It was always so quiet—a grandparents' neighborhood if there ever was one.

"Chriiiiistopher! Dinner!" His mother's voice floated up the stairs, along with the delicious smell of chocolate cake. He galloped downstairs, taking two steps at a time, and burst into the kitchen to find his grandmother waiting for him, hands on hips.

"Not even going to say hello, eh?" she said with a mischievous twinkle in her eye. She had a soft Scottish accent, and red hair just like his mother's.

Christopher smiled sheepishly. "Hi, Nana. Sorry . . . I just wanted to put my stuff away, that's all. How're you doing?"

"Fine, thank you very much for asking. Now sit down and eat."

Mr. and Mrs. Wice spent the night and headed home the next morning. After they left, Christopher followed his grandfather out to the garage to talk about the work that needed to be done.

In Papa's garage, like his father's, everything had a place. Seeing a loose screwdriver on the workbench, Papa carefully hung it on the wall rack before turning to Christopher.

"Well, our two toughest projects are going to be putting new topsoil on Nana's garden out back, and repainting the garage door. You think you might be up to all that?"

"No problem. I came here to work, Papa. Just tell me what you want done, and I'll do it."

Papa nodded approvingly. "That's the spirit. I hope you brought some old clothes that can get dirty, though." He glanced doubtfully at Christopher's baggy skateboarding jeans. "I'd hate to see your, um, *good clothes* get ruined."

Christopher laughed. "Don't worry, I brought some old work clothes. When we're done, we can just burn them."

Later, the teenager would remember those words.

## A DAY OFF

Christopher worked side by side with his grandfather over the next few days. They turned over dirt in the backyard, and weeded until Christopher's hands were stained green. Then they cleaned the garage and painted the door. The garage took longer than Christopher thought it would, nearly all day. By Tuesday, they both decided to take a break.

Christopher slept late, then got up and dressed in clean clothes. It felt good; his work clothes were getting really crusty.

He had decided to take the subway into Toronto for the day. There were lots of good places to skate there, and he didn't get to go very often. He stuffed deodorant and an extra shirt into his backpack, grabbed his skateboard and bolted downstairs.

The aroma of freshly brewed tea met him halfway. He smiled, knowing what to expect. Sure enough, Papa was sitting at the kitchen table, reading the paper and drinking his hot tea.

"I'm leaving now," Christopher said, "but I'll be back in time for dinner."

Papa put down his tea. "Do you have money for lunch? And for the subway trip home?"

"I'll just eat something cheap at Taco Bell. I've got enough for that."

The old man glanced over his shoulder to make sure his wife wasn't listening. "Here," he whispered, pulling out his wallet. "Take some extra just in case." He shoved a few small bills into Christopher's hand.

"Wow, thanks!" Christopher said.

"Shh! I don't want your grandmother to catch me. She and your mother are always after me about giving you grandkids money."

Christopher shoved the money deep into his pocket.

"Well, I like it," he confided in a low voice. "In fact, you can slip me money whenever you want. I won't tell, promise."

Papa winked. "You'll think you've earned every penny by the time we finish with Nana's garden tomorrow. Better have fun while you can!"

## SKATER'S PARADISE

Downtown Toronto was a skateboarder's paradise. There were buildings with large, open courtyards, and sidewalks that ran in a big circle. When Christopher arrived there that afternoon, about fifteen skaters were already practicing.

"Hey, what's up?" they greeted him in a chorus. He didn't know most of them, but it didn't matter. Soon he was in the middle of the crowd.

None of them talked much while they were skating. It took a lot of concentration to jump a board onto a curb or rail, grind it, then land it smoothly. The only sounds other than passing traffic were the clatter and hum of skateboard wheels—and an occasional surprised yelp when one of them fell.

By late that afternoon, Christopher was sweaty, bruised, and starving. As he collapsed into his subway seat, two words were on his mind: dinner and sleep.

It was almost seven o'clock when he trudged up the front steps of his grandparents' house. It took a huge effort just to pull open the front door. He didn't remember it being so heavy.

"Nana! Papa! I'm home!" he called. Too tired to carry anything upstairs, he tossed his skateboard and backpack into the hall closet and wandered into the kitchen.

"Nana?"

The kitchen was empty . . . not a good sign. His stomach was now grumbling loudly. He glanced out back, then checked the garage.

"Ah, Christopher!" his grandfather greeted him. He was standing in the garage sorting through gardening tools. "Have you had your dinner yet?"

"No. Had tacos for lunch, but that was a long time ago. Where's Nana?"

"She went shopping. By the time you get cleaned up she should be back." Papa looked with satisfaction at the clear workbench. "It looks like we'll have to go out in the morning and buy bags of soil and fertilizer for the garden. Are you still up to the job?"

Christopher was so tired that he didn't even feel up to climbing the stairs. But he nodded anyway. "Sure. I'll be ready whenever you are." He didn't want his grandfather lifting those heavy bags by himself.

After dinner, Christopher sprawled on the living-room couch and watched skateboarding videos until bedtime. He was glad he'd spent the day doing something exciting. One thing was sure—spreading dirt in his grandmother's garden the next day would be b-o-r-i-n-g.

The house was quiet when Christopher woke the next morning. He blinked at the clock on the nightstand. It was ten-thirty. He stumbled downstairs, his stomach once again growling.

"Nana?" he called in a sleepy voice. "Nana? Papa?"

No one answered. Christopher wondered for a moment if his grandfather had had another heart attack during the night. But if so, wouldn't Nana have woken him?

Then he heard someone pulling into the driveway. Peeking out the front window, he saw that it was his grandparents.

"Hey, where were you guys?" Christopher demanded as they came up the steps. They were both carrying small shopping bags.

"We went to the mall," Nana replied briskly. "Your grandfather needed some gardening supplies. Why?"

"Oh, nothing . . . I just wondered, that's all. Is there anything that needs to be carried inside?"

Papa nodded. "We bought some big bags of soil. I'll need your help bringing those in." He was wheezing a little from walking and climbing the steps.

"I'll go get them," Christopher offered quickly. "You don't sound like you're breathing too well today."

The old man shook his head in frustration. "Let me tell you, it's no fun getting old. Every day it's something else." He lowered himself onto the living-room couch to catch his breath.

Christopher started for the door, but his grandfather waved him back. "Hold on. That dirt isn't going anywhere. Have you had your breakfast yet?"

"No." Christopher yawned hugely. "That's a good idea. I'll grab something to eat, then take a quick shower to wake up."

"You should wait and shower after we finish spreading all that dirt. You'll just get filthy again."

Christopher shrugged. "Okay."

He had no way of knowing that his life—and the lives of others—would soon hinge on that simple decision.

"So we're dumping all the dirt into the garbage bin?" Christopher stood in the garage, cradling a lumpy bag of garden soil in his arms. He had changed into a green golf shirt that his mother liked. He planned to ruin it before the day was out.

His grandfather nodded. "It'll be easier than carrying the bags out one by one."

"I'm all for easier," Christopher said. He ripped open his bag and began to shake the dirt into the bin. His grandfather patted his shoulder, then bent to pick up another bag.

"Papa, let me do that. You know you shouldn't be lifting something that heav—"

*KA-BOOOM!* An earsplitting noise drowned out Christopher's words, even his thoughts. To his astonishment, the garbage bin seemed to explode in front of him, blowing the dirt up into his face. Above him, the roof of the garage popped open like the top of a jack-in-the-box, then came crashing back down at an odd angle. Christopher caught a glimpse of his grandfather a few feet away. The old man's shirt was dirt spattered, his face gray with shock.

The next few seconds seemed to pass in slow motion. As the thunderous noise went on, the floor beneath their feet began to tremble. Screwdrivers, hammers, and other tools clattered off their racks and rained down on them. Christopher tried to scream, but his mouth was full of mud. The deafening rumble made his chest vibrate.

"Papa!" he finally sputtered. He took a stumbling step forward, then watched in horror as a thick wood beam swung down from the ceiling and hit the back of his grandfather's head.

The old man swayed, but didn't fall. His gray hair turned red with blood as he waved Christopher to his side.

"Keep your head down!" he shouted, hunching his body over Christopher's like a human umbrella. "Come on, we've got to get out of here!"

The ground was still shaking as they ran for the garage door. It was twisted and bent, hanging down by its hinges. As Christopher peered out, a piece of twisted metal hit the driveway and rolled a few feet. Splintered wood and shards of broken glass rained down on the roof above them.

What was *left* of the roof above them.

"What's going on?" Christopher cried. "Papa, what's happening?"

Abruptly, the strange rumble began to die down. "I don't know." Papa looked dazed, his white undershirt stained with blood. "Maybe lightning struck the chimney and it fell onto the garage. Come on!"

Together, they ran outside.

## A BLACK CRATER

Christopher's relief at escaping from the garage vanished as soon as he reached the driveway. Next door, where a nice house had stood just minutes before, there was only a smoking crater. He stared in openmouthed horror.

Slowly, other sights and sounds broke through his shock. All down the block, people were screaming and running into the street. Water spewed from broken pipes, and a sharp smell burned his nostrils. As he stared, the whole side of another house fell away, revealing a bedroom and hallway. Hunks of wood, glass, and metal were scattered for as far as he could see. In the distance, he heard a baby crying.

With all the noise and confusion, Christopher barely heard his grandfather muttering in shock: "Our house . . ." When he turned to look, he was stunned. The gray two-story was nothing but a huge pile of rubble!

Christopher stared, the image of the broken house burning itself into his mind. The roof was caved in. The walls had tumbled in on all sides. The whole second floor had collapsed onto the first floor. Bricks, wood, and twisted metal stuck out everywhere.

*Nana!* The thought struck Christopher like a blow to the stomach. Behind him, Papa gasped.

"Your grandmother's in there!" he said frantically. "We've got to get her out!"

His words stung Christopher into action. "I'll get her, Papa. You go help the neighbors!"

Before the old man could protest, Christopher raced toward the house. The front porch was cracked and broken, with knifelike shards of glass scattered everywhere. Christopher's pulse pounded in his temples, his breath coming in short gasps.

He dashed up the broken steps, then glanced back. His grandfather, still dazed, was stumbling toward the next-door neighbor's house, blood running down the back of his head.

Christopher jerked open the front door.

At first he couldn't see or hear anything. The air was thick with sawdust, and his heart was pounding so hard that it made a throbbing sound in his ears.

He cupped his hands around his mouth. "Nana!" he yelled. "Nana, where are you?"

The sawdust clogged his throat and made him cough. He stumbled forward into the front hallway. The walls were cracked and caved in. A huge piece of the roof was hanging down like a curtain. He cocked his head in different directions and strained his ears, hoping to hear something—anything— from his grandmother.

"Nana?"

The floor was covered with splintered wood and other junk. Nails were sticking up everywhere. Christopher waded through the wreckage, heading for the living room. That was the last place he'd seen his grandmother.

"Nana? Yell if you can hear me!"

Then he heard it—a faint cry. "Over here!"

It came from somewhere just ahead. Christopher squinted to see through the sawdust haze. Where the living-room couch should have been, there was a jumbled stack of wooden beams, drywall plaster, and shingles. Where was she?

"Nana, say something! Keep talking!"

For a moment there was no reply. Christopher was starting to panic when he heard another weak cry: "Under here!" Nana's voice sounded like it was coming from the heap of rubble over the couch.

The teenager moved fast. Kicking chunks of wood and plaster aside, he used his hands to fling other pieces aside. "I'm coming, Nana!" he shouted encouragingly. "I'm almost there! Just hang on!"

He forced his way into the living room, then shouted again: "Nana? Say something so I'll know where you are!"

"Under here. I'm under here!" She was sobbing now.

Christopher suddenly felt scared and dizzy. He'd never heard his grandmother cry before. This couldn't be happening. What if he couldn't get to her in time? The thought left him frozen, unable to function. Her muffled sobs filled the thick air.

Then his grandmother whimpered, "Christopher?" The faint cry jerked him back to reality.

"I'm right here, Nana," he said, trying not to let

his own voice quiver. "I'll have you out in a second. Everything's going to be okay."

He reached the spot where he thought his grandmother was buried. How could she breathe under there? Bending down, Christopher clawed at the junk covering her. Sharp edges and splinters ripped his palms, but he didn't even notice. He had to get to her—fast!

The small stuff was easy; he tossed that to one side. But there were several heavy wooden beams that just wouldn't budge. Christopher pushed and strained, but it was no use.

*They're too heavy,* he thought in despair. *I can't lift them!* He stared at the huge, splintered beams. What was he going to do? He had to concentrate!

Then he saw a small movement deep in the rubble. He was so close to freeing Nana; he *had* to do it! With renewed determination, Christopher grasped the top beam and heaved. A burning feeling shot up through his arms, and his straining muscles felt like they might burst. Inch by inch, he raised the heavy beam until it was chest-level. Then, realizing he was holding his breath, he exhaled and gave one last mighty heave. The beam toppled to one side.

Sawdust flew everywhere as Christopher stood gasping for air. He could see his grandmother more clearly now, lying crumpled on one side.

"Nana!" he panted. "Can you move now?"

"I think so." Slowly, painfully, the elderly

woman crawled out through the small opening he had cleared. Her shirt and slacks were torn and dusty, and her eyes were glazed with pain. Christopher helped her stand up.

"What happened?" she asked, looking around hopelessly. Her once-beautiful house looked like it had been bombed. She held her right wrist close to her body. "My house . . ."

Christopher shook his head. "We don't have time for that, Nana. We've got to get you out of here!"

She looked confused. "But—"

"Come *on*!" Christopher put his arm around her and urged her forward. "I think I smell smoke."

The moment he said it, he knew it was true. He glanced around wildly. Where was the smoke coming from? Was that what had happened to the house next door? Did something catch on fire and explode?

The thought sent a thrill of fear down his spine. He glanced around at the destroyed living room. If the house caught on fire with them still inside . . .

Breathing fast, Christopher practically carried his grandmother over the piles of rubble. She was too dazed to resist. His heart beat louder and louder in his ears, like the countdown on a time bomb: *Boom, boom . . . Boom, boom . . . Boom,* boom!

Finally, they reached the front door. "We're almost there," Christopher said. "Just a few more steps, Nana!"

A second later, still holding his grandmother

firmly, Christopher staggered outside. He rushed her down the steps, ignoring the broken glass that crunched underfoot. He didn't stop running until they reached the front sidewalk.

Outside, a crowd had already gathered in the street. As Christopher panted to a stop, his grandfather rushed up. He could hardly breathe.

"Are you all right?" he gasped. "Are you hurt?"

Nana shook her head in bewilderment. "I don't think so. What happened?"

Christopher breathed deep, letting the clean air fill his lungs. It felt good. It felt safe.

Papa pointed to where the house next door had once stood. "People are saying a gas furnace blew up, but I don't know. It's crazy."

Just then a shriek went up from the street. "Fire! *Fire!*"

Christopher, Nana, and Papa all turned to gaze back at the broken shell of their house. At first it was just a bright orange flicker through a broken upstairs window. Then, with a loud *whoosh!,* a fiery column shot straight up into the sky.

Within seconds, the whole house was a sea of flames.

A fierce blast of heat seared their faces, forcing them farther out into the street. Nana put a trembling hand to her mouth. "It's gone," she said. "Everything's gone." Turning blindly, she buried her face in Christopher's dirty shirt and burst into sobs. He patted her back helplessly.

In the distance, sirens began to wail. An army of fire engines, ambulances, and police cars arrived and blocked off their street. Overhead, a news helicopter circled, dipping low for a better view. Paramedics and firemen worked frantically to free an elderly woman in another house who was pinned underneath a refrigerator.

*That could've been Nana,* Christopher thought numbly. He hugged her tighter.

Firefighters quickly moved in, aiming half a dozen high-speed hoses toward Nana and Papa's house. The water created giant steam clouds as it hit the flames. The heat was so intense, it could be felt half a block away.

Watching the water flood the house, Christopher couldn't help but think that just half an hour earlier, he'd planned to take a nice, long shower. If he hadn't decided to wait, he would've still been upstairs when everything exploded.

Back in Barrie, Colleen Wice was standing on a stepladder scrubbing walls. It wasn't exactly her idea of a good time, but someone had to do it. When the phone rang, she yelled, "Steven! Can you get that?"

Her husband didn't answer. Exasperated, she jumped off the ladder and grabbed the phone. "Hello?"

"Mum! This is Christopher. There's been a huge explosion! Papa and Nana's house—" Suddenly, with a crackle, the phone line went dead.

Colleen stood rooted, staring down at the phone. Something had happened to her parents! She could tell by Christopher's voice that he wasn't kidding around.

She jumped when the phone in her hand rang again. "Christopher?" she shouted. "Is that you?"

"Yes! Listen, I'm using some guy's cell phone, and it's going dead. The house next to Papa and Nana's house . . . it blew up! Papa and Nana's house . . . it's . . . it's . . ."

"It's what? Christopher, tell me what's happened!"

"It's gone! Their whole house is gone!"

Colleen looked up as her husband walked in. "Get the keys, Steven. We're leaving!"

Christopher sat alone in a police trailer, waiting for his parents to arrive. After all the excitement, he felt numb and exhausted. He squeezed his eyes shut, trying to block out everything, but the events of the past hour kept rushing through his head.

The only part of Nana and Papa's house left standing was the chimney. Their once familiar neighborhood looked like a war zone, with shattered windows and streets littered with wet papers and broken furniture. A toilet was sitting on top of one roof. The air was thick with smoke.

A helicopter had landed on the street a few minutes earlier to airlift the woman who'd been stuck under the refrigerator. Another woman had been treated for minor injuries.

"She was blown out of a second-story window," one of the policemen told him. "Right through the glass and all."

Nana and Papa were on their way to the hospital. It looked like Nana's wrist was broken and Papa's head might need stitches . . . but they were alive.

Christopher felt a lump rising in his throat. He had come so close to losing them. Before he could stop himself, he burst into deep sobs.

## OLD COINS FOR A NEW BOARD

For weeks after the explosion, Christopher remained nervous. He refused to go anywhere upstairs or into a basement. He even had panic attacks where he would start trembling and not be able to move.

The nightmares, however, were the worst—reliving the explosion over and over in his dreams. Each time he woke up, sweating and scared, he determined to "get over it." But it wasn't that easy to do.

The thing he wanted most was to get back to a normal life—skating with friends, practicing new tricks. The only problem was, he didn't have a skateboard, even an old one, anymore. His board had been destroyed along with everything else in Nana and Papa's house.

Then one day Papa called to say that he had a job for him.

"You know all those coins I used to save in that

big jar? The jar melted in the fire and the coins got charred black, but they can still be spent. If you'll clean them up for me, I'll give you a percentage of the money.''

"Sure!" Christopher said. "Thanks, Papa!"

The old man chuckled. "Better wait to thank me until you do the work. It's going to take a wire brush and oven cleaner to get that black mess off."

It took almost two weeks. But when the last coin was bright and shiny, Papa counted them, then handed Christopher two hundred dollars.

"I hear," he said with a smile, "that there's something you've been wanting to buy for a long time. Think this might be enough?"

Christopher looked up at him, his eyes suddenly bright. "A Birdhouse board," he breathed. "Yeah, it's enough."

*This story was submitted by YTV Achievement Awards in Toronto, Ontario, Canada.*

"Papa" and "Nana" McLaughlin,
March 1996.

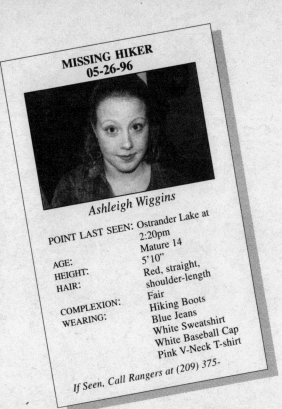

**MISSING HIKER**
**05-26-96**

*Ashleigh Wiggins*

| | |
|---|---|
| POINT LAST SEEN: | Ostrander Lake at 2:20pm |
| AGE: | Mature 14 |
| HEIGHT: | 5'10" |
| HAIR: | Red, straight, shoulder-length |
| COMPLEXION: | Fair |
| WEARING: | Hiking Boots |
| | Blue Jeans |
| | White Sweatshirt |
| | White Baseball Cap |
| | Pink V-Neck T-shirt |

*If Seen, Call Rangers at (209) 375-*

# Lost Hiker

## THE ASHLEIGH WIGGINS STORY

"**O**kay, what if someone was bleeding really bad?"

Ashleigh Wiggins eyed her friends, Beth and Megan, across a jumble of empty Girl Scout cookie boxes. When neither of them answered, she said impatiently, "Well?"

Megan rolled her eyes. "Why is it that every single one of these questions ends with me ripping up my shirt? Can't there be even *one* where I just dial 9-1-1 like everybody else?"

"Yeah, really," Beth said, laughing. "What about that drowning question a minute ago? Couldn't you just grab a stick to help the drowning person instead of throwing your clothes out to pull them in? I mean, if I'm wearing a brand-new silk shirt or something, they're just gonna have to drown!"

Ashleigh smiled and pushed back her thick red hair, tossing the Girl Scout handbook toward the boxes. "I think they meant if there weren't any sticks or things around. I don't think you're supposed to say, 'Oh, an emergency! Quick, let's rip our clothes to shreds!' "

Megan reached for the book, still giggling. "If I have to answer one more 'what if' question, I'm going to keel. I mean it, too."

Ashleigh, who was fourteen years old, had known Megan and Beth since fourth grade. In seventh grade, they had decided to form a small Girl Scout troop. They met twice a month to talk, eat junk food, and work on various projects to earn Girl Scout badges.

"I've got to go, anyway," Ashleigh said. "I've got play practice for *Her Majesty, the King,* and a million lines to have memorized by tomorrow."

Beth groaned. "You know you had your lines memorized before anyone else even started. I bet you already know the whole thing by heart!"

"Not yet," Ashleigh said with a grin, getting her stuff together. "I don't like to depend on somebody else to cue me if I forget. It makes me feel stupid."

Piggie clattered through the kitchen to the pig door and raced toward the doghouse with Freckles, the Australian shepherd, hot on her heels. Ashleigh peeked out the window. As usual, the potbellied pig was in the doghouse, and the dog was under a shady bush, glaring.

Piggie had come first, and she hadn't been happy when the dog joined the household. In protest, she sometimes ran off—usually to sprawl on the cool garage floor, or to bury herself in the compost heap.

"Hey, guess what?" a muffled voice called from behind two big bags of groceries. The bags plopped down on the kitchen counter, revealing Ashleigh's mom, Janice. "We're going backpacking in Yosemite next weekend!"

Ashleigh sat down and put her head on the table, silently groaning. Her mother knew she *hated* hiking. Really hated it.

"Sorry, Mom," she said, trying to *sound* sorry. "I have Tech Weekend, so I can't go. I've got to help build the sets and check the sound and lighting." Ashleigh glanced at her mother's face, trying to see if her good-daughter ploy was working. "I've got to get my costume, too."

"You know Tech Weekend isn't required, Ashleigh," her mother said firmly. "Nice try, though."

"I really, *really* don't want to go, Mom."

"That's really, *really* too bad, Ashleigh."

Ashleigh's father, Paul, wandered into the kitchen in time to catch the last exchange. He worked in a slaughterhouse as a meat grader for the USDA.

"If you're talking about Yosemite, remember that Bridalveil Creek floods a lot in June," he commented. "We'll have to cross it on the way up."

"Yes," said Janice, "but this isn't June. It's May. I'm sure it'll be fine."

"Mo-om!" Ashleigh whined. "Next weekend is the *last weekend* in May, right? It's practically June."

"We'll be fine, guys."

Ashleigh sighed. She knew her mother, and once she made up her mind, it took dynamite to change it. At least this time, though, she had given them a week's notice. Other times, she had announced on a Friday morning that they were going camping, and expected them to be packed and ready by noon.

Ashleigh wandered into the living room dejectedly, kicking at the carpet and trying to remember what line in the play came after, "Do we always have to eat gooseberry jam? Doesn't our Kingdom raise *any* strawberries?" She poked a finger into the cage that held Big Bird and Kermit, the parakeets. They looked very cheerful.

"You're only smiling because you don't have to go, birds. You're lucky they don't make little boots small enough for your feet. Or teeny little backpacks, either. Mom would have you out on the trail in no time."

A whirlwind of curly red hair blew into the room. "Did you hear we're going *camping*?" Bonnie, Ashleigh's little sister, asked excitedly.

"Yes," Ashleigh said shortly.

"I can't *wait*! And Melanie gets to go *with* me!"

Bonnie's enthusiasm got on Ashleigh's nerves.

"Oh, goody. Why don't you run along and tell all your little friends what a great time you're going to have fighting off spiders and getting blisters? That sounds like *soooo* much fun, Bonnie." Being an actress, Ashleigh flung her arms wide, adding a dramatic touch.

Bonnie glared and stomped out, probably to call Melanie, their cousin. Bonnie was always talking, either on the phone, or to the pig if nobody else was around. She was a certified "talkaholic."

Ashleigh went to her room and looked around for something—anything—to cheer her up. She spotted her Girl Scout Interest Project book under a pair of dirty jeans. She mentally shrugged. She might as well make the camping trip worthwhile. Maybe she could earn a Girl Scout badge out of the ordeal.

Flipping through the handbook, Ashleigh read the list of requirements for the backpacking badge. Mostly it was brain-numbing things like "Learn about the most common water pollutants in the area," or "Show that you understand the principles of minimal-impact camping." Gag.

Then she found one about assembling a first aid kit. That sounded easy, especially since she knew her mom already had a first aid kit. She'd just take hers.

"Yes!" she said, checking it off. "Well, that was easy." She flopped back on the bed, glancing at the drama masks hanging on her bedroom walls. They reminded her of her drama project. She was supposed to write and direct a scene that would be performed at school in a few weeks.

Pulling out a notepad, Ashleigh began to scribble. She had already decided to make her scene about four crazy people in a mental institution. Her main characters were going to be an ex-gym teacher named Hewitt, who taught too many years of PE and couldn't stop blowing his whistle; Jeremy, a man who had a pearly white smile and loved brushing his teeth so much that he named his toothbrush "Charlie"; and two more crazies. She hadn't decided who they'd be yet.

She frowned, trying to conjure up two nice, easy-to-write-about crazy people. Nothing came to her. She finally gave up and pulled out a book she'd been reading. *Follow My Leader* was an old paperback about three Boy Scouts who went camping and got lost. It was one of her favorites, passed down from her grandmother.

But for now, she couldn't settle down to read. Her lines in the school play kept nagging at her. Her role as Countess Stephani was originally a guy's role. *Count* Stephani was described as "a large man, nearing sixty, and pompous in every movement." Ashleigh had to turn it into a girl's role, which made some of the lines sound funny. She pulled out her beat-up script and spent the rest of the evening rehearsing her role.

• • •

Saturday morning dawned bright and sunny. Ashleigh sighed as she looked out her bedroom window. She'd been hoping for thunderstorms or blizzards. Anything to cancel the camping trip.

Jackie, the cat, jumped up on her bed. Ashleigh tickled her under the chin.

"Why is it," she asked the cat, "that the weather never cooperates? When you want sunshine, it pours. And when you want a storm, you get nothing but sunshine?"

Jackie blinked—a cat version of a shrug—then turned to stalk away across Ashleigh's bed. Deciding it was pointless to talk to a cat's behind, Ashleigh started packing. When she heard her mother in the hall, though, she leaped up and popped her head out of the door.

"Mom, I'm *not going!* You hear me?"

Her mother just laughed and disappeared into her own bedroom. She didn't even bother to answer.

"Well, I guess I am," Ashleigh said to Jackie, who had turned to face her again. Ashleigh glumly jammed jeans, shirts, underwear, and a hairbrush into her backpack. She also wedged in her book. Maybe it would inspire her while she was stuck in the Great Outdoors.

She reached for her makeup kit, then hesitated. Why bother? Who was going to be out there to impress anyway—a raccoon? She dropped the makeup back onto the dresser. If she was grouchy, she might as well be ugly, too.

She zipped her pack closed and dragged it into the kitchen, where her mom was busy packing snacks for the trip. Ashleigh peeked over her shoulder. It would be at least some consolation if they got to eat junk food all weekend.

But no. Instead of chocolate bars and potato chips, her mother was packing some icky-looking cranberry things and banana-flavored granola bars! Ashleigh made a puking sound, which her mother ignored.

"No way I'm going to eat *those*, Mom!" she said. "Why'd you buy them?"

"They looked good." Her mother strapped a sleeping bag onto the outside of her pack, then shoved the whole bundle into Ashleigh's arms. "Carry this out and put it in the trunk for me, okay?"

Ashleigh refused to be distracted. "Gross dried-up old cranberries," she said sulkily. "Probably poison someone."

She stomped out to the car, her face set in a scowl. Behind her somewhere she heard giggling. Sure enough, Bonnie and Melanie bounced happily past her, carrying their backpacks. By the time Ashleigh reached the car, the two little girls were already bouncing their way back into the house.

Ashleigh gritted her teeth. How could *anyone* be excited about walking uphill with a heavy pack strapped to their back? Ashleigh decided Bonnie must be crazy. Maybe she should make her one of the crazy people in her play.

She stuffed her mother's pack into the trunk ungracefully, still musing. Hiking . . . crazy people . . . it all fit together. She'd have to give it some thought.

Ashleigh slammed the trunk and turned back toward the house. Maybe, she thought hopefully, something would happen at the last minute to make everyone stay home. She glanced up at the tree in the front yard. What if she fell and broke her leg? That would do it!

But then she couldn't be in the play next weekend. "Break a leg!" was a common saying in theater, but they didn't mean it literally.

Okay, forget the broken leg. How about a nice sprained ankle? She looked around the yard, but didn't see any good holes to step into. It would have to be convincing to work. After all her complaining, her mom would think she was faking no matter what she did.

It was hopeless. She was going.

While she'd been standing there, Bonnie and Melanie had rocketed back and forth several more times, still giggling. Ashleigh suddenly noticed that none of her father's camping gear was being loaded.

"Wait a minute!" she called. "Where's Dad's stuff? He's still going, isn't he?"

Her mother hurried out with another armload. "He's not feeling well. We're going to have to go without him this time, I'm afraid."

Bonnie and Melanie were already in the car with their seat belts buckled. "Let's *go*!" Bonnie yelled.

Janice Wiggins smiled. "Okay, okay. Come on, Ashleigh."

Ashleigh trudged to the car, glaring through the window at her sister. At least she got to ride in the front seat . . . not that it would make her feel any better about being kidnapped for the weekend.

It was a going to be a long, long drive to Yosemite National Park. That is, if *she* had anything to do with it!

Ashleigh spent most of the drive staring out the window, refusing to talk. She resisted her mother's efforts to cheer her up.

"Here, read this," Mrs. Wiggins said, handing her a colorful park brochure. "This is going to be great. You'll see."

The brochure showed a bunch of cheerful camping people. After one disgusted look, Ashleigh thrust it away. Her mother got the idea and finally left her alone.

They reached the trail head a little before noon. The hiking trail led away up the mountain, marked by old license plates painted bright yellow and nailed to the trees. Sighing heavily, Ashleigh got out and shouldered her backpack. They were all loaded down pretty heavy, since they had to carry their tent, sleeping bags, food, water, and clothes.

Mrs. Wiggins locked the car and waved toward the trail. "Let's go, ladies!" she said cheerfully. "If we keep moving, we should be able to make it all the way up to the lake before dark. It's a great place to camp."

"Yeah, right," Ashleigh mumbled.

Once they started walking, though, Ashleigh didn't waste any time. She sped ahead of the others. The woods were quiet—that is, as long as she stayed far away from Bonnie—and the ground was springy and damp. Ashleigh found herself humming after the first few minutes.

Maybe this wasn't going to be so bad after all.

After an hour or so, Ashleigh pulled off her sweatshirt and tied it around her waist. To keep her mom from worrying, she scratched notes in the dirt or snow whenever she stopped to rest, writing brilliant things like: "Ash," or "I'm Over Here." Then she went a short way into the woods to sit on a log and read. She was a big fan of sitting around.

She stayed ahead on the trail until her stomach started growling. She glanced at her watch. Lunchtime! Since her mom had all the food, Ashleigh decided to wait for her to catch up.

She heard Bonnie's shrill voice long before she saw the little group straggling up the trail. When they came in sight, Ashleigh waved and yelled, "Over here!" Bonnie and Melanie ran up to her, both grinning.

"Are you guys hungry?" Ashleigh hoped the answer would be yes. Her mother had been known to hike for days without eating. Well, maybe not days, but for many, many hours. She was really into the whole outdoors thing.

"I'm starved!" Bonnie exclaimed. "Mom! Can we stop for lunch now?"

Ashleigh smiled fondly at her little sister. Every now and then she made herself useful.

"Good idea!" Janice Wiggins responded. She shrugged out of her pack, then dug around in it until she found some slightly squashed sandwiches. She passed them around, then handed out bags of chips. They all found rocks or logs to sit on while they ate.

Ashleigh wolfed down her sandwich. Everything tasted better when you ate outside—or maybe it was just that you were always half-starved before you got to eat.

By the time she finished, though, she was shivering again. She pulled her sweatshirt back on. The damp log she was sitting on was also getting uncomfortable. She was glad when her mom announced that it was time to get moving again.

Ashleigh stayed with the family this time, a decision she regretted as soon as Bonnie and Melanie started singing. They picked a song from the movie *Pocahontas* ("All of my life I've dreamed of a land like this one"). Ashleigh rolled her eyes. It was one thing to hike uphill with a heavy backpack, but another thing entirely to hike uphill while being forced to listen to a song about loving the land!

"Hey!" she interrupted. "Why don't we sing the Tarzan song instead?" Without waiting, she led into it, singing at the top of her lungs:

"TAR-zan! Swinging on a rubber band . . . TAR-zan, fell into a frying pan . . . Ooh, that burns! Now TAR-zan has a TAN!"

Soon Bonnie, Melanie, and even her mom were belting out the words:

"JANE! Cruising in an airplane . . . JANE, crashed into a freeway lane . . . Ouch, that hurts! Now JANE has a pain, and TAR-zan has a TAN . . . !"

Each verse had hand and body motions that went with it. Ashleigh beat on her chest as Tarzan, fluffed up her hair as Jane, and made monkey motions when they got to the verse about "CHEE-TAH!" It was one of those songs you had to know if you were a Girl Scout; it was practically required.

By mid-afternoon, as they continued to climb, the snow patches became deeper and deeper. Ashleigh still thought it was kind of crazy to go camping in the snow. Still, she had to admit—at least to herself—that she was starting to enjoy herself.

By six o'clock, Bonnie and Melanie were whining that their feet hurt and that they were starving. Ashleigh was tired and hungry, too, but she was glad the little girls had said it first.

"All you do is *whine*," she said smugly, enjoying being the *non*-whiner for a change. "Bunch of little babies." Bonnie glared at her, and Ashleigh stuck out her tongue. It might not be mature, but it felt good!

The sun was going down as they passed another family's campsite along the trail. They already had a lantern hanging from a tent pole. Janice Wiggins finally motioned their group to a stop.

"It's another two or three miles to the lake," she said, "but it doesn't look like we're going to make it tonight. Let's just make camp here, along the trail. We can hike up to the lake first thing in the morning and leave all the heavy stuff at camp."

"Great idea," Ashleigh said, dropping her heavy pack with a thud. She was in favor of any decision that meant she could sit down.

The two little girls collapsed on the ground, exhausted and begging for food. While her mother set up their camp stove and put water on to boil, Ashleigh wrestled with their hexagon-shaped tent. Once it seemed sturdy, she picked out the softest spot and spread out her sleeping bag inside.

Their dinner "menu" for the night included hot tea and dehydrated chicken soup. With snow on the ground and a deep chill in the air, anything hot sounded great. After Bonnie revived a bit, she wandered over to the camp stove.

"Can I dump in the soup mix, Mom?" she begged.

The water was just beginning to boil. "Sure," Mrs. Wiggins answered. "I'll get it."

Bonnie ran to get Melanie, but as she turned, she accidentally bumped the hot stove. It slid sideways, knocking over the pot. Boiling water splashed on Bonnie's leg.

"Ahhhhhhh!" the ten-year-old shrieked, trying to shove the hot stove away from her. "Mo-om!"

Ashleigh and her mom both ran over to help. When they pulled Bonnie's wet pant leg up, her skin was bright red and already swelling.

"I'll get some snow," said Mrs. Wiggins. "Ashleigh, you get out the first aid kit."

Bonnie was wailing. Ashleigh felt sorry for her; the burn on her leg looked bad. She pulled out the first aid kit and rummaged through it, looking for burn cream or bandages.

"It's going to be okay, Bonnie," she said soothingly. "Just hang on." Unfortunately, the first aid kit didn't have a lot in it. Ashleigh suddenly wished she had gone down the Girl Scout checklist like she was supposed to.

Her mother ran back with a handful of snow. "This will help," she said as she pressed it onto the burn. Bonnie whimpered with relief as the snow melted against her hot skin.

Once Bonnie calmed down a little, Ashleigh dressed her burn the best she could with a small gauze pad and a tube of cream. She also gave Bonnie some aspirin.

"Thanks, Ash," Bonnie whispered.

"No problem. Listen, you want me to read to you for a while? This is a really great book." Ashleigh pulled out her battered copy of *Follow My Leader*. Maybe it would take Bonnie's mind off her burn. She flipped through the pages, looking for an exciting part.

"Here we go," she said. "Okay, here's the story. These three Boy Scouts are out on a camping trip, and they decide to go down into this valley to watch the sun come up, or go down, or something. One of the boys, Jimmy, is blind, so he brings his guide dog along. The dog's name is Leader. When they're ready to go back to camp, they suddenly realize they're lost. They get into this big argument about which way to go."

Bonnie was listening, her face still tear-streaked. "What happens?" she asked.

"Well, Jimmy—that's the blind boy—says he has an idea. And since they're lost, the others decide they have nothing to lose."

Clearing her throat, Ashleigh began to read:

*All right, the others agreed.... Which way, Jimmy?*

*For an answer, Jimmy took hold of the handle on Leader's harness and said firmly, 'Leader, take me home. Home, Leader!'*

Ashleigh read on, watching Bonnie out of the corner of her eye. Listening to the story seemed to make her feel better. She kept reading until her mother called out that dinner was ready.

They ate as the sun went down. The air quickly turned icy, so they went to bed early. Bonnie and Melanie fell asleep the moment they were stuffed into their sleeping bags. Ashleigh took out her contacts, then wiggled into her own sleeping bag. She could hear laughter and voices from the people at the next campsite. There was also a creek bubbling somewhere nearby.

She read *Follow My Leader* by flashlight for another hour or so before drifting off to sleep.

Smoke. Something burning.

In her sleep, Ashleigh wrinkled her nose, but the choking smell finally woke her up. Harsh morning light was shining in through the little screen window on the side of the tent. She blinked, her mind working slowly to identify the burning smell.

Pancakes. That explained it; her mother was cooking. Ashleigh relaxed, then groped around for her contacts. Maybe the world would look better today once she could see it.

Sure enough, when she poked her head out through the tent flaps and got her first whiff of pine trees, mountain air, and torched pancakes, she felt unusually cheerful. Even when her mother handed her a plate of semiburnt pancakes, oozing with real maple syrup instead of the fake syrup that she liked, she smiled.

Bonnie woke up whimpering. "Mom, I want to go home. I don't feel like walking. My leg hurts."

Mrs. Wiggins hesitated. "Honey, we're going to have to walk whether we go up or down . . . and we're less than two miles from the lake. I think you'll feel better once we get up there. It's really beautiful, you know."

Ashleigh gave Bonnie some more aspirin after breakfast. Since they were leaving their camp set up, the only pack they needed to take was the one with food and water. Ashleigh grabbed it. It would give her a place to carry her book.

This time, Ashleigh stayed with the others. She felt a little sorry for Bonnie as she limped along. They made extra stops to let her rest, and each time, Ashleigh read two more pages of *Follow My Leader* aloud.

It was a steep climb. Since they had camped right at the snow line, the higher they went, the thicker the snow became. It took nearly three hours to reach the lake. After lunch, Bonnie and Melanie went over to talk to some other kids who were exploring the area. The lake was a popular camping spot. Ashleigh decided to wander around and take a look for herself.

She didn't find much of interest except for a small wooden lodge. She tried the door, but it was locked. She walked around the corner to find her mom leaning against the lodge, talking on her cell phone.

Ashleigh rolled her eyes. Talking on the phone in the middle of the wilderness! Didn't that kind of defeat the purpose?

"Mom! Who're you talking to?" she asked rudely.

Her mother ignored her, but Ashleigh eavesdropped long enough to figure out that it was her dad. They had tried to call him the night before, but her mom's cell phone hadn't worked down in the trees. From the way she had it pressed against her ear, it probably wasn't working too well even now.

Ashleigh finished reading *Follow My Leader,* then wandered around for another few minutes. Finally, she crunched her way through the snow over to her mom.

"I'm bored. I'm going back to camp now to start dinner, okay?"

Mrs. Wiggins was watching Bonnie and Melanie as they played around by the lake. "Okay, sweetie. Just be careful and watch the trail. We'll be right behind you."

Ashleigh grabbed the small backpack again and started down the trail. It was easy to see their footprints from the trip up. She also watched for the yellow license plates that marked the trail.

After about an hour, though, the trail grew slushy, making the old footprints harder to see. Ashleigh was so busy watching the ground that she almost tripped over a fallen tree when she hurried around a bend.

She stopped and looked around. Where was the next marker? She frowned and looked again, turning in a slow circle. Then she saw the missing yellow marker—on the fallen tree!

Ashleigh squinted at the tree for a minute, trying to figure out which way the marker would've pointed when the tree was still standing. She couldn't really tell.

"Some mountain woman I'd make!" she said aloud, kicking an icy clump of mud. She backed up for a minute, trying to guess which direction the trail continued from the last three markers. Because of the bend in the path, it was impossible to tell.

Finally, she spotted what looked like faint, slushy footprints leading away from the fallen tree on the other side. *That must be the trail.* She hurried forward.

Her feet were cold, and her stomach was starting to growl. She couldn't wait to get back to camp and eat. She planned to make camp pizza. The others would be lucky if there was any left for them!

The footprints became harder and harder to see. In some places, they were just small dents or melted places in the snow. It wasn't until Ashleigh reached a patch of snow that was clean, totally unmarked by footprints, that she halted again, confused.

"How'd I get off the trail?" she asked nobody in particular. She peered ahead, then back, looking for the yellow markers. She didn't see a single one. An uneasy feeling stirred in her stomach.

"Okay, don't panic," she said. "This is no big deal." She considered going on a little farther to see if she could find the next marker, but decided against it. No way was she going to get lost in the woods. Unlike the Boy Scouts in her book, she didn't have a guide dog to take her home!

Disgusted, she trudged over to a large, flat rock and sat down to think. Her mom had said she'd be following with the girls in a few minutes. Ashleigh decided to wait for fifteen minutes and see if they showed up. If the slowpokes didn't catch up by then, she would just follow her own footprints back up the trail and meet them halfway.

She leaned forward, propping her elbows on her knees. She wished now that she hadn't finished her book up at the lake. Fifteen minutes was a long time to sit without anything to do. She glanced at her watch, then looked around the woods. Yep, lots of trees. Still.

Her behind was getting cold.

What did other people do while they were waiting? In books they always twiddled their thumbs. She tried it. That took up about four seconds. Good job.

She looked at her watch again. Only seven minutes had gone by. She didn't have enough patience to wait another eight minutes. She jumped up and slapped her numb behind, trying to warm it up.

"Well, I've had about enough of the great outdoors," she told the trees. "I'm outa here."

She hitched the backpack higher on her shoulders

and started confidently back in the direction from which she'd come. Following her own footprints, she could return to the last marker she'd seen. By the time she got there, surely her mom would be on her way down.

But when she tried to find her footprints from seven—now eight—minutes before, she couldn't see them. The ground was all slush.

"Oh, great!" Ashleigh exclaimed, throwing her hands in the air. "Just great. First the stupid markers disappear, and now my footprints vanish. Where'd they go?"

She spun around quickly once, then turned in a slow circle, checking every inch of the ground carefully. She *thought* she had come from *that* direction, but now she wasn't really sure. She walked that way for a few minutes, then stopped again. Once again, she was facing a patch of pure, clean snow.

Her heart thudded heavily as she realized that she had taken another wrong turn. The "trail" after the fallen tree must have been a game trail made by a deer or something.

She was lost.

The first shock left Ashleigh's heart pounding. She spun in a circle to pick a good direction to scream. She decided one was just as good as the other, since she had no idea where she was.

"Mom!" she bellowed. "Mom, where are you? Can you hear me?"

She waited a second for an answer. Nothing.

"Bonnie? Melanie?" she shouted. "Anybody . . . ?" The woods around her remained silent. She started to feel sick to her stomach. "Hey! Somebody come get me!"

She yelled her lungs out until her voice grew hoarse. By then she was so upset that it was hard to breathe.

"No one can hear me," she said numbly. "I'm out here in the middle of nowhere, and nobody can hear me. I'm in big trouble here."

She leaned back against a tree, then slid down the trunk until she was sitting on the ground. She pulled her knees up to her chest and began to cry.

"Mom!" she sobbed. "Come find me!"

Bonnie and Melanie raced giggling into their campsite, expecting the smell of dinner cooking. Bonnie stared in surprise; the fire hadn't been started, and the little camp stove was still closed and cold.

"Ashleigh?" she called, glancing around the quiet camp. "Where are you?"

Janice Wiggins came down the path a few steps behind them. "What's the matter? Where's Ashleigh?"

Bonnie shrugged. "I dunno. Maybe she's off hiding somewhere. And she hasn't even *started* on dinner!"

Her mother frowned. "Go check the tent to see if my pack is there."

Bonnie poked her head through the tent flaps. "Nope!"

Her mom put her hands on her hips. "Ashleigh!" she yelled into the trees. "Stop fooling around. Where are you?"

When Ashleigh didn't jump out, laughing, Bonnie and Melanie looked at each other, knowing something was very wrong.

Ashleigh had never made it back to camp.

Ashleigh took a shuddering breath and wiped her eyes with the back of her hand. Her stomach hurt from crying, and her head was pounding.

*What was she going to do?*

It took a few minutes for her to calm down and start thinking straight. She was a Girl Scout, trained to deal with emergencies. She should be able to deal with this.

*I wish I'd paid more attention to some of those survival questions,* Ashleigh thought miserably. There had to be some way she could get back to civilization. But how?

She squeezed her forehead with her hand, trying to make her brain think harder. What had she learned that could help her out of this mess?

Well, one thing was for sure. This was one situation where ripping up her clothes wouldn't do any good! If she wasn't back at camp by the time the sun went down, she was going to freeze.

• • •

Bonnie sat outside the tent, staring up at the sky. It was getting colder and colder, and Ashleigh still wasn't back. Her mom had just left for the lake again to look for her. She was trying to act like everything was okay, but Bonnie could tell she was worried.

She got up and wandered over to help Melanie with dinner. They poked at the canned stew that was bubbling on the camp stove. The wind was picking up. They had heard from some other campers that it might even hail that night.

Ashleigh only had one sweatshirt with her. How was she going to keep warm?

Ashleigh was still trying to come up with a plan when she noticed a faint bubbling sound nearby. She sat up straighter, suddenly hopeful.

"The creek!" she exclaimed. "That's it!"

She remembered hearing the creek the night before. It must run close to the trail where they'd camped. All she had to do was find the creek and follow it downhill. It should lead her "home" to their campsite.

And even if I miss our camp, she thought cheerfully, I can follow the creek down to Yosemite Valley. There were always lots of people there. She could send someone back up the mountain to find her mother.

She smiled, feeling much more in control of the situation. She struggled up to her feet, then decided to sort through her mother's backpack before she started walking again. She was hungry. Maybe her mom had hidden some *good* snacks in there.

Unzipping the pack, Ashleigh squatted next to it and dug around. There were four full water bottles, a water filter, four banana-flavored granola bars, half a bag of shriveled cranberries, and some Oreo cookie crumbs. *Small* crumbs.

"Way to go, Mom," Ashleigh muttered in disgust.

She kept digging. Her mom's gloves . . . Bonnie's overalls . . . paper . . . the first aid kit that didn't have much in it besides aspirin and Band-Aids. There was also some money for emergency phone calls, a sewing kit, a bottle of hand lotion, and some Benadryl.

Oh, goody.

Ashleigh drank some water, then sat back to puzzle over which, if any, of the items she could use. She wasn't in a sewing mood, and she *hated* banana bars and cranberries. Unless she ran across a convenient pay phone in the woods, the phone money wouldn't help. Why couldn't her mother have packed useful things, like candy bars and a Walkman?

"Oh, well, deal with it," she told herself, sounding scarily like her mother. She'd have to watch that in the future.

She heard the rushing creek very faintly in the distance. It was hard to tell exactly which direction the sound was coming from, but Ashleigh decided to get started. It was cold, and getting darker every minute.

She trudged off through the snow and slush, angling toward the noise. She had only taken about twenty steps when her feet suddenly slipped out from under her. The next thing she knew, she was flat on her back, staring up at a tree.

"Ow!" she yelled in surprise, half from pain, half from the chill of the ground. It was so icy and wet, she had a hard time getting a foothold anywhere to stand back up.

Now she was not only lost, but wet and muddy. Angrily, she stomped toward some clean snow. At least it would be better than walking on ice.

As her feet started to sink deeper and deeper into the snow, though, she found herself struggling with each step. After a while, the snow came up past her knees.

"Stupid snow!" she screamed in frustration. She wasn't getting anywhere! After struggling in what seemed like slow motion for a long time, Ashleigh was in tears again. Her feet felt frozen and heavy, like pieces of wood.

She finally stopped, too tired to go on. "Why me?" she shouted. "I didn't want to come on this stupid trip to begin with!"

Then, in the trees just ahead, she noticed a strange root. It grew straight up out of the ground, and went across, then back down, almost like a kneeling altar at church. Seeing it reminded Ashleigh of something her youth pastor at church had said a few weeks before.

"If you ever find yourself in deep trouble," he had told her youth group, "get down on your knees and pray. You might be surprised at what happens."

Now, staring at the root altar, Ashleigh realized that she'd never been in a deeper trouble than this. She stumbled over and knelt on top of the root.

"Please, God," she prayed aloud, "get me out of here. I want to go home! You know I belong to you, and I'm thinking you probably want me to go home. I'm scared out here by myself, so please help me."

It was strange, but as soon as she finished praying, she felt calm. Even though she was still alone in the woods, she didn't *feel* alone.

With a lighter heart, she hauled herself back to her feet. It was time to start moving again.

Bonnie strained her eyes, watching the trail leading up toward the lake. Her mom should be back any minute. She had said she was going to call for help if she didn't find Ashleigh up at the lake. Bonnie had a terrible feeling that Ashleigh wouldn't be there.

It would be dark soon. Where was her sister?

• • •

Ashleigh had just stumbled upon an odd little marsh, where spikes of dead grass stuck up from a muddy trickle of water.

"A baby creeklet," she muttered. "Maybe it'll get bigger as it goes downhill."

She followed the trickle down the mountain, hoping it would lead to the main creek. She remembered that they had camped to the right of the creek, so she stayed on that side. If this was the same creek, she should run into their campsite soon.

After walking for what seemed like miles, though, the trickle didn't seem to be getting any bigger. She kept hoping that she would come around a bend and see—the big creek! Her mom! Their tent! Practically anything but what she *did* see, which was more trees, more snow, and the same pathetic creeklet she'd been following for miles.

*This is like being trapped in a maze of trees and ice,* Ashleigh thought. *I don't know which way to go, or even if this is the same creek that runs by our campsite! If it's not, I'm probably miles off the trail by now.*

The thought sent a shiver through her. "Well, Ash," she said aloud, "it's too cold to stand around feeling sorry for yourself. Take yourself home!"

Clenching her cold fists in her pockets, she forced herself onward.

• • •

"Mom!" Bonnie jumped up and ran to meet her mother. "Did you find her?"

"No," Janice Wiggins replied shortly. "I called 9-1-1 from up at the lake and told them that Ashleigh's missing. They said they'd get together a search team right away, and send a park ranger up here to talk to us. If Ashleigh doesn't turn up soon, they'll start a full-scale search at dawn."

Bonnie's eyes grew wide. "At *dawn?* You mean tomorrow morning? What about tonight?"

Mrs. Wiggins blinked back tears. "They said—they said the chances of finding her up here at night aren't all that good. I called your dad. He's on his way."

As the sky darkened and the wind grew colder, Ashleigh continued to follow the tiny, winding creek. Finally, she noticed that the sound of rushing water was getting louder. She hurried around the next bend, then gave a joyful whoop. A big, *fat* creek stretched out in front of her, over twelve feet wide and moving fast!

"Yes!" she yelled. "I made it!" Despite the chill breeze, Ashleigh felt warm with triumph. Now all she had to do was find their campsite.

She hurried forward, determined to get "home" before dark. Her mom was probably hysterical by now. Ashleigh grinned, picturing how relieved everyone would be when she strolled into camp. This would make a great story to tell the drama class on Monday!

A moment later, though, her smile faded. Directly ahead, *another* big creek angled in from her right to join the creek on her left, cutting her off. To keep going, she would have to cross one of the creeks.

Ashleigh knew she hadn't seen anything like that on the way up to the lake. This wasn't their creek at all.

Down in the parking lot in Yosemite Valley, a park ranger scribbled a short note, then stuck it under the windshield wipers on Janice Wiggins's car. When emergency calls came through, the lost person often ended up back at the car.

The note said simply:

*ASHLEY—*
*YOUR MOTHER HAS NOTIFIED US BY CELL PHONE THAT YOU ARE MISSING FROM YOUR CAMPSITE.*
*PLEASE WAIT HERE WITH THE VEHICLE. RANGERS WILL CHECK THE AREA TO LOOK FOR YOU.*
*THANKS,*
*JOANNE GILL, PARK RANGER*

Ashleigh stumbled along beside the creek, looking for a place to cross. It was getting almost too dark to see.

Snow patches lined the creek bank, and the grass along the edges was crusted with ice. She stared out at the dark, rushing water, trying to find a spot that looked shallow. It was going to be cold.

She picked a place to cross, then stopped long enough to peel off her sweatshirt. She didn't want it to get wet. Still, she hesitated at the edge of the water. It looked cold.

Just get it over with, she told herself. If you think about it too long, you'll never do it!

She plunged one foot, then another, into the creek. The water was so cold that it hurt, and the current almost knocked her off her feet. It took her a few seconds to get steady enough to walk across. By then her feet were already numb.

Ashleigh gritted her teeth and forced herself forward. The icy water swirled over the tops of her knees, and then up to her thighs. She waded across as quickly as she could. By the time she reached the other bank, her teeth were chattering. She crawled out, grabbing roots to help steady her.

Standing up, then walking, was hard. Her legs were numb and shivering, and her wet jeans felt like a straightjacket. She staggered up the slippery bank to more level ground, then dropped her pack. She had to get out of her wet clothes and get warmed up—fast! She knew from Girl Scouts what frostbite could do to fingers and toes.

Too cold to feel self-conscious, Ashleigh quickly scraped off her soaked tennis shoes and socks, then unzipped her jeans. It was hard to get them off, especially with both her hands shaking with cold. Once her jeans were off, she pulled back on her shoes and her dry sweatshirt.

Her arms were warmer, but her bare legs were blue with cold. She rummaged around in her mom's pack again, hoping to find something warm.

What she really needed was a pair of warm sweatpants and some dry socks, but all she found was a pair of her little sister's overalls. Desperate, Ashleigh stuck her legs into them and tried to force them up over her hips, but there was no way. Then she tried to rip them along a seam, but they were sewn too well. She finally threw them back into the pack and started walking along in her underwear.

In the near-darkness she tripped a lot, and thorn bushes tore at her bare legs. Still, she hurried on. She was no longer convinced that she knew where she was, or even that she was going in the right direction, but something inside kept urging her forward.

ASHLEY —

Your MOTHER HAS NOTIFIED US BY CELL PHONE THAT YOU ARE MISSING FROM YOUR CAMPSITE —

PLEASE WAIT HERE WITH THE VEHICLE. RANGERS WILL CHECK THE AREA TO LOOK FOR YOU —

THANKS —
JOANNE GILL
PARK RANGER
5/26    1730

*Find a safe place to spend the night.*

The thought cut clearly through Ashleigh's misery. She nodded, almost as if in response to a spoken command. Night was closing in around her. She couldn't keep walking when she couldn't see.

She slipped again, this time pitching forward onto her knees. Something sharp ripped her right knee. She grabbed her bare leg. It was sticky with blood.

"Oh, great," she moaned, rocking with pain. "Just what I needed." The skin on her legs was ice cold and prickled with goose bumps. She wished again that she had some dry pants.

The gash on her leg was too big for a Band-Aid. Ashleigh folded her damp sock into a pad and pressed it hard against the bleeding cut. She held it there until she grew too chilled to sit on the ground any longer in her thin underwear. She had to find shelter for the night before she froze, or hurt herself even worse.

She limped a little farther before coming upon a small clearing. Two fallen trees were crisscrossed over some rocks, making a snug little cave. She decided to stop.

The wind was picking up. Ashleigh took the time to spread out her wet jeans to dry before she crawled into the shelter. She curled into a shivering ball, pulling Bonnie's small overalls over her legs for warmth.

Bonnie sat up sleepily, hearing voices outside the tent. It was her mom, talking to a ranger.

"We've got search and rescue people hiking all the main trails," the ranger said. "If your daughter just wandered off onto the wrong path, they'll find her."

Janice Wiggins's voice sounded strained. "I should never have let her walk back by herself. If anything's happened to her . . ."

"Don't even think about that yet, ma'am," the ranger said soothingly. "She probably just took a wrong turn. We've got professional trackers out there who can follow any trail. We'll find her."

Bonnie heard a low rumble of thunder in the distance. It made her heart sink. What was Ashleigh going to do if it started raining?

It was cold. *Really* cold. In her tree shelter, Ashleigh felt a fresh crop of goose bumps popping out all over her body. She had just dozed off, but something had awakened her.

Then she heard it again—thunder. She huddled into a tighter ball. The scanty branches above her wouldn't even begin to keep out rain. And if she got soaked . . .

She would freeze to death.

The thought wasn't as scary as it would have been hours earlier. Now, as cold and miserable as she felt, death sounded almost peaceful. Hypothermia would set in and she would slowly fall asleep. The trouble was, she would never wake up.

Ashleigh shook herself, angry that she was letting

her thoughts go there. In the movies, they always said to stay awake and keep moving. That might work great during the day, but she'd already found out what happened when she kept walking in the dark. She'd end up falling off a cliff or breaking her neck on some rocks.

The wind picked up, blowing damp raindrops into her shelter. Ashleigh scooted as far under the logs as she could. Her stomach was shivering, and she could no longer feel her feet. She was already half-frozen.

Then, without warning, it began to hail. As marble-sized hailstones rattled violently against the logs above her, icy rain seeped in through every crack.

"Stop it!" Ashleigh cried hysterically through blue lips. "I can't take any more!"

Janice Wiggins stepped out through the tent flaps and stood huddled in her coat, looking out at the dark trees. It was almost four o'clock in the morning now, but she couldn't sleep. The violent hailstorm that had just passed through had brought terrible images to her mind; Ashleigh, wet and freezing in the darkness, Ashleigh, sobbing with fear.

Alone. Lost.

*Please, God, be with Ashleigh,* she prayed for the millionth time. *Protect her from the cold, and from wild animals.*

The loud snap of a twig behind her sent her whirling around in a panic. She almost shrieked before she recognized the tall figure looming out of the darkness. It was her husband!

"Paul!" Mrs. Wiggins cried, rushing to him. "I didn't expect you until daylight!"

"I started hiking up at midnight," Mr. Wiggins said quietly. "I would've been here earlier, but I missed your camp the first time. Some trackers up the trail told me how to find you."

Bonnie stirred inside the tent, thinking she was dreaming. She heard her father's voice . . . but he hadn't come with them this time. She moaned and rolled over, burying her face in her sleeping bag. She'd been having a really bad dream about Ashleigh. . . .

Ashleigh woke up suddenly, not knowing until then that she'd been asleep. At first she didn't remember where she was, but the darkness and cold soon reminded her. She held her watch up to her face, wondering how long she'd been asleep.

"An hour?" she said out loud, exhausted. She hoped she could sleep longer than that before waking again.

Miserable and shivering, she dozed off for a few minutes at a time. Each time she woke, she would check her watch. After a while she had to stop looking, because it seemed like the night would never end.

It was almost dawn when Ashleigh woke up

again. She must have been dreaming about the hike up to their campsite the day before, because she had the song from *Pocahontas* stuck in her brain. She didn't even know all the words, but she found herself humming it. For some reason, it cheered her up.

The sky outside was turning a lighter shade of gray, but the air was still freezing. Ashleigh decided to stay awake until the sun came up. Maybe it would warm her up.

To keep herself occupied, Ashleigh tried singing the *Pocahontas* song: "All of my life I've dreamed hm-hmmm-hmm, hm thiiis one!" It kept her mind off other things. She sang the same words—the only ones she knew—over and over again through numb lips.

The next thing she knew, she was waking up again, only this time warm sunshine was touching her cheek. It gently warmed her frozen face, then crept through her body. After a long night of shivering, the cramped muscles in her arms and legs slowly began to relax.

The sunrise was beautiful, sending orange-red streaks across the sky, but Ashleigh didn't notice. She had finally dropped off into a deep, sound sleep.

The Search and Rescue teams were ready at sunrise. The park rangers told Paul and Janice Wiggins to pack up and go down to the command center to wait for news. They didn't want to leave their campsite, just in case Ashleigh found her way back, but the searchers said that it was the best idea.

Bonnie and Melanie trudged silently down the trail, following the adults. When they reached the bottom, Paul Wiggins paused and looked back up at the mountain. Tears began to stream down his face.

Bonnie ran over to take his hand. He sat down on a log and pulled her up next to him. Together, they wept.

It was noon when Ashleigh woke again. She sat up groggily, thinking she'd heard a dog barking somewhere nearby. Had she dreamed it? She wasn't sure.

"Maybe it's a rescue dog," she said. Her voice sounded hoarse. She wasn't sure if it was from the cold, or from singing "Pocahontas" ninety times. She pulled out a water bottle and took a sip, straining her ears in case she heard another bark. If it was a rescue dog, she needed to start screaming or something.

Then she had another thought. Rescue dogs weren't the only things on the mountainside that could bark. What if it was a wolf, or a coyote? She wouldn't want to draw *their* attention by screaming!

In the end, it didn't matter. She didn't hear another bark.

After sitting very still for a while, listening, Ashleigh decided that she was finally hungry enough to eat one of the granola bars, even if they *were* banana-flavored. If she was going to get out of this alive, she had to keep up her strength. She forced herself to chew and swallow half a bar, then washed it down with stale water. If somebody didn't find her soon, she'd need to filter some fresh drinking water from one of the creeks.

The little bit of food helped. It was time to get moving again. She quickly gathered her things, and pulled back on her jeans, shoes, and socks. They weren't dry, but she put them on anyway. She'd already found out how sharp the rocks and bushes could be. Her legs were crisscrossed with cuts.

With food in her stomach and the sun high in the sky, Ashleigh felt more optimistic than she had since she'd first realized she was lost. By now, surely people were out looking for her. Her mom would've seen to that!

Thinking about her mother made Ashleigh feel guilty for getting lost, but she quickly pushed the thought aside. She didn't have the time or energy to worry about that right now. She needed to concentrate on getting out of this mess!

She knew now that the creek she'd been following wasn't the same as the one they'd camped by. Could it be Bridalveil Creek? If so, she was still okay. All she'd have to do was follow Bridalveil down until it reached the falls. She'd been there before. There was a hiking trail leading straight down from the three hundred-foot falls into the valley.

When she reached the creek, though, she got a nasty surprise. Somehow, *another* big creek had sneaked in during the night, because now she could see it on her right. She was stuck back in the middle between creeks again!

"I am Job," she said aloud, referring to a Biblical character stricken with many bad things at once. "I'm cursed. I'll have to cross another stupid creek!"

Then she saw a log lying like a bridge across the water. Relieved, she crawled across it to reach the other side. Her clothes were almost dry now, and she wanted to keep them that way.

She hiked for a while, then stopped to filter some drinking water. Squatting next to the creek, she stuck the filter tube into the water and pumped until her bottle was full again.

As she jammed the filter back into the pack, she caught a glimpse of something bright blue. She fished it out, then laughed. It was a pad of Cinderella notepaper!

"Well, that's useful," she said. "Let's see . . . who should I write a note to?" Then she had an idea. If people were out searching for her—and she hoped sincerely that they were—she could leave a note by the creek to tell them which direction she was going.

She pulled out the pencil stub and wrote in big letters: "I'M LOST. I'm walking downstream on the right side of this creek. Ashleigh Wiggins, May 27th."

Now where should she put it? There was a huge, flat rock sticking out over the water. Ashleigh spread out the blue paper and used a smaller rock as a paperweight. She stepped back to see how it looked. It was certainly eye-catching!

She continued downstream.

Bonnie was waiting with her parents, listening to the rescue people radio in. No, they hadn't seen Ashleigh. Several of them said, "Not even a trace." What was *that* supposed to mean?

They had sent helicopters out to look for Ashleigh. Bonnie could see them in the distance, circling different areas of the woods. The park rangers had also printed up a "Missing Hiker" flyer with Ashleigh's picture on it. They were passing them out to everyone in the park.

Seeing the "Missing" flyer with her sister's face made it all seem worse.

Ashleigh had just spotted a familiar landmark off to her right: Glacier Point, a giant rock sticking up from a mountain peak. She had been to Glacier Point with her family before, and she remembered the trail there. A nice, big, *marked* trail.

She had planned to follow the creek all the way down, but if she could cut across to Glacier Point, she'd be unlost. After a moment's hesitation, Ashleigh decided to leave the creek and go for it.

She hiked cross-country, walking as fast as she

could. The closer she got to Glacier Point, though, the thicker the brambles got. She had to push her way through the thorny brush. Finally, it got so bad that she gave up and turned back toward the creek.

Trudging along, Ashleigh wondered how she'd gotten herself into this. Some Girl Scout she was! If she'd been lost in a mall, she would've known exactly what to do: stay in one place and wait to be found. Come to think of it, that's probably what she should've done in the woods, too, but she hadn't thought of it at the time. Now she was so far from the original trail that nobody would think to look for her here.

It was a chilling thought. She remembered hearing about search parties that were called off after a week or two. Everybody thought the person was dead, so they stopped looking. What if that happened to her?

*Please,* she thought, *please keep looking for me.*

"Why can't anyone find her?" Janice Wiggins asked tearfully for the hundredth time. "There are helicopters flying everywhere, and searchers on all the trails. Where else could she be?"

A park ranger shook his head. "Girls usually stay close to where they first get lost, but it's beginning to look like Ashleigh kept moving. If she would just stop somewhere—anywhere!—we'd have a better chance of locating her."

Mrs. Wiggins leaned against her husband. "Ashleigh always wants to do everything by herself. I don't think she'll stop and wait for help."

Ashleigh let out a joyful whoop when she saw a bright yellow trail marker dead ahead.

"It's a trail!" she screamed. "A trail, a trail, I've found a trail!" She danced around with excitement for a second. An hour, maybe less, and she'd be back with people!

She started down the winding path, keeping a close eye on the markers. She'd learned her lesson about *that*! Soon she reached a junction with three signs, and three trails leading away.

Two of the signs said VALLEY, but one said 7 MILES TO VALLEY and the other said 8.5 MILES TO VALLEY. That was an easy choice. Ashleigh picked the shorter trail.

The feeling of *not* being lost anymore put a bounce in her step. She sang the Tarzan song several times, then decided to use the rest of her time alone to practice her lines for the play. After all, tomorrow was play rehearsal.

"But, Your Majesty—if you will pardon me—this is very serious. . . ." In her role as Countess Stephani, Ashleigh raised her chin high and made a sweeping gesture in the air. "To break off the match now . . . it is an almost unforgivable insult!"

Her voice rang out loud and clear in the forest as afternoon slowly turned to evening.

Two hours later, Ashleigh was too tired to speak,

much less sing. She just wanted to get home, take a shower, and eat some real food. The cut on her leg was throbbing, and her stomach was cramping from hunger. She was getting almost desperate enough to eat the banana granola bars.

She was hurrying, almost running, hoping to get out of the woods before dark. Suddenly, the trail opened out into a large burned area. The trees there were all charred, and the markers, if there were any, were burnt beyond recognition. Ashleigh stopped, stunned.

"No!" she screamed. "Why does this keep happening to me?" The trail was gone, and by the time she climbed back up the steep mountainside to reach the junction again, it would be dark. It didn't make sense to go back.

Somewhere off to her left, she heard the creek bubbling. Ashleigh headed for the familiar sound. It took a few moments for another, different, sound to register.

A helicopter.

"Wait!" Ashleigh said. She looked around in a panic, realizing that she was hidden by the trees. She ran for the nearest open area and started waving her arms. "I'm over here!" she screamed. "Hey, helicopter! This way!"

The helicopter headed straight for her. Ashleigh grabbed Bonnie's overalls from her pack and waved them above her head, thinking they'd be easier to see. She waited for the pilot to signal in some way.

Instead, he flew straight over her head—and kept going.

Ashleigh's jaw dropped. "Come back!" she shrieked. "Are you blind? I'm right here!"

She kept screaming and waving until the helicopter disappeared behind the trees. By then the sky was almost dark.

When the search was called off for the night, Bonnie got upset. "Mom, Ashleigh's still out there!" she said. "They can't just stop looking for her. What if she's hurt or something?"

Her mother's eyes were red and puffy from crying. "I know, honey. But in the dark they could miss her, and some of the rescuers could get hurt. They'll start looking again first thing in the morning."

As Bonnie sat listening to the adults talking, all she could think was that Ashleigh might be out there somewhere freezing, or bleeding to death, or surrounded by wild animals.

*Please come home, Ashleigh,* she said silently.

Ashleigh stumbled on, hardly looking where she was going. How could the pilot have missed her? Was she invisible, or what?

The creek seemed to go on forever. As the sky darkened again, Ashleigh realized that she would have to spend another night in the woods. She stopped when she saw what looked like a tiny cave between some rocks.

Her feet were swollen and aching as she crawled into the small opening. She took off her shoes, then chewed part of a loathsome banana bar. Her stomach was knotted with cold and hunger.

The night passed in a miserable blur.

An irritating *thumpa-thumpa* sound woke Ashleigh late the next morning. In a daze, she looked up to see a helicopter sweeping along just above her. She jumped up, screaming.

"Stop! I'm right here!" The helicopter kept going. "Come back! Please!"

When it disappeared, Ashleigh realized the searchers couldn't see her. She must be a tiny speck among all the trees and rocks. She was on her own.

She rubbed her eyes, wondering why everything looked so blurry. That's when she discovered that she'd lost her left contact lens.

"Great," Ashleigh said aloud. "What's next? An avalanche? A forest fire? Give me a break!"

She didn't even bother to look for the missing lens among the rocks and pine needles. With a sigh, she shouldered her pack and started off again.

It was now Tuesday. She was missing play rehearsal. That thought upset Ashleigh almost more than being lost. She thought of all her friends sitting in school right now, nice and bored, while her own desk was empty. She never thought she'd be upset about missing school!

Over the next few hours, helicopters flew past her five or six times. Ashleigh waved and yelled each time, but she didn't have much hope that they would see her.

They didn't.

*I'm going to get out of here,* she thought, growing more stubborn with each step. *I don't need helicopters. Or searchers. Or food. Or warm clothes. I might have to walk a hundred miles, but I'll get out of here!*

Two steps later, she saw the men across the creek.

"They found her!"

The park ranger yelled the news to the crowd of friends and family who had come to wait with the Wiggins family. "One of the search parties just radioed in to say that they found her, and that she's all right!"

Bonnie stood still, letting the news sink in. Everybody around her started shrieking and hugging each other. Her mother ran over and grabbed her up in a big hug.

"Ashleigh's okay!" she said. "Can you believe it, honey? She's okay!"

Bonnie finally nodded. "I'm glad," she said. For once, she couldn't think of anything else to say.

At first, the blurry glimpse of a man wearing a bright yellow vest left Ashleigh wondering if she was imagining things. Then she saw other yellow-vested people milling through the trees.

*Rescuers!*

"Hey!" Ashleigh screamed, cupping her hands around her mouth. "Hellooo! Yo, I'm over here!"

The first man she had seen looked up. An amazed expression spread across his face. "Are you Ashleigh?" he shouted.

Ashleigh almost gave a smart answer like, "No, I'm George!" But she answered simply, "Yes!"

Across the creek, the men started jumping up and down and cheering like they were at a football game. Ashleigh was surprised to find that tears were rolling down her cheeks.

She was found. She wasn't alone anymore.

"Sit down and stay put!" the first man yelled. "We're going to go down the river until we find a place for you to cross."

Ashleigh, still crying, did as she was told. She felt like she was in a dream when, a few minutes later, the men helped her cross the creek one last time. When she came out of the freezing water this time, though, there were people waiting to help her into warm, dry clothes.

"There's a helicopter not far from here," one of the rescuers said. "Your family's going to be very excited to see you, young lady!"

By the time they reached the helicopter, Ashleigh was too grateful to complain about all the times they had flown right past her. Somebody handed her a bright yellow jumpsuit to put on, and one of the rescuers pressed something into her hand. Ashleigh glanced down to see a banana-flavored granola bar.

"I know you must be starving," the man said kindly. "Go ahead, eat it."

Ashleigh thought about the four unopened banana bars she still had left, then smiled.

"Thanks!" she said sincerely. And she ate every crumb.

ABOVE: Ashleigh coming off the rescue helicopter to join anxious family and newspeople. AT LEFT: The reunion—Ashleigh, Mom, and Dad.

(Photos by Fresno Bee)

# Crushed by a Car!

## THE STORY OF FIVE AMAZING KIDS

ABOVE: "The Rescue Team,"
Gordon, Omar, Shuggie, Tamika, Raymond.

The loud blast of a truck horn outside sent ten-year-old Omar Turner running to the living-room window. His eyes widened when he saw a U-Haul truck roll to a stop in front of the house across the street.

"Shuggie!" he yelled. "Somebody's movin' into the downstairs at Raymond's house!"

Shuggie, who was eight years old, quickly joined his older brother at the window. "You seen any kids, or is it just old people?" he asked. "I hope they've got kids."

Omar shrugged. "I dunno. Let's watch for a minute and see."

Their patience paid off when a teenage girl and younger boy appeared and walked to the back of the U-Haul truck. A woman followed, pointing toward the house.

"They *do* have kids!" Shuggie said gleefully. "I bet that's their mom. Let's go talk to them."

The boys were halfway to the door when their mother, Karla Turner, spotted them. "Hooooold it!" she sang out. "Where do you two think you're going without coats? It's cold out there!"

"Oh, Mom," Omar grumbled. "We're just goin' to say hi to the new kids across the street. There's a boy who looks about my age."

"Really?" Mrs. Turner peeked out the window. "Well, I guess you can go over for a minute, but you be polite, you hear me? And don't get in the way."

"C'mon, Omar," Shuggie said. They both grabbed jackets and ran outside.

It was early December in Denver, Colorado. On this Saturday afternoon, with the sun shining and the sky blue, it didn't *look* cold. When they stepped outside, though, the wind sweeping down from the mountains was icy.

Omar and Shuggie weren't usually shy, but as they crossed the street, they both felt a little awkward. What if the new kids didn't *want* to meet them? What if the mother was mean? What if—

A familiar voice interrupted their thoughts. "Omar! Shuggie! Wait up!" Raymond Brown, thirteen, waved from his upstairs doorway, then ran down to meet them. His house was divided into three living areas, one on each floor.

"Hey!" Omar greeted him. "What's the deal with the new people moving in downstairs?"

Raymond shrugged. "I dunno. My mom says she met them a couple weeks ago when they were looking at the house, but I wasn't home. You going to talk to them?"

"Yeah."

Raymond nodded. "I'll come with you."

The two younger boys quickly fell into step with Raymond. One of the oldest kids on their street, Raymond was a good basketball player. He also had a black belt in tae kwon do.

The woman had disappeared into the house by the time they reached the U-Haul, but the two kids were still standing outside. Raymond walked up to them with a confident smile.

"Hi!" he said. "I guess you're our new neighbors. I'm Raymond, and this is Omar and Shuggie."

"I'm Gordon," the boy said. "Oh, and this is my sister, April. She's sixteen."

"How old are you?" Omar asked curiously. "I'm ten. Shuggie's only eight." He ignored his little brother's glare.

"I'm almost ten," Gordon replied proudly. "My birthday's next month."

Raymond smiled. "I've got a little sister who's nine. She'll probably be over here bugging you in a while."

April nudged her brother impatiently. "C'mon, Gordon. We need to start carrying stuff in, or

Mama's gonna yell at us.'' She lifted a cardboard box out of the U-Haul.

Omar looked doubtfully from the truck filled with boxes to Gordon. ''You need any help?''

Gordon's face lit up. ''Yes! But I guess you'd better come meet my mom first.''

Omar sighed. Meeting moms wasn't one of his favorite things. Raymond jabbed him in the back.

''Let's go,'' Raymond said, answering for all of them. They followed Gordon up the steps and into the house, single file.

Trina Stevens, Gordon's mother, was busy wiping out the cabinets and drawers in the kitchen. When the four boys trooped in, she looked up in surprise.

''Well, hello there!'' she said. ''Who do we have here?''

Gordon introduced the others. ''They said they'd help us carry in stuff,'' he said. ''Is that okay?''

His mother laughed. ''Are you kidding? We can use all the help we can get!''

As the boys headed for the door, Mrs. Stevens lightly patted the top of Shuggie's head. The eight-year-old squirmed in embarrassment. Moms were always patting his head or kissing him. Sometimes it was hard being the littlest.

Back at the U-Haul, they decided which boxes to move first. Omar stepped up to take a box, then slapped his forehead. ''Man, I forgot!'' he said.

"Shuggie, we're not supposed to be lifting heavy stuff."

Gordon looked puzzled. "Why not?"

Omar sighed. "Me and Shuggie were in a car accident a couple months ago, and now we have to go to physical therapy all the time. Mama's gonna skin us if she sees us lifting boxes."

"What kind of accident?" Gordon asked. "What happened?"

This time Shuggie answered. "We were riding with my dad when some guy smashed into our car. It made our necks hurt bad. We have to take Tylenol all the time now."

Omar made a face. "I really hate it. Every time we play football, I end up having to ask Mama to rub Icy Hot on my neck . . . then she yells at me to quit playing football and basketball. But I don't want to change my whole life! It's not fair."

"That's pretty bad," Gordon said sympathetically. "Maybe you'd better not help."

"No, we'll do it," Omar said quickly. "We'd better just carry the lighter stuff, though. Mama'll be mad if we both come home wanting Tylenol and Icy Hot!"

That settled, the four new friends started unloading the truck.

## A FORBIDDEN GARDEN

"Raaaay-mond! Can I play?"

Nine-year-old Tamika Brown stood on tiptoe to yell, as if that would make the boys hear her better. Raymond, Omar, Shuggie, and Gordon had taken a break from moving boxes to play a quick—and noisy—game of street football. Mika had heard them and run outside.

Raymond puffed to a stop next to his sister. "No," he answered shortly. "Besides, I think we're done."

Omar sauntered over, holding the football over his head. "We are the champions! How's it feel to *lose*, Raymond? Hah!"

Raymond gave Omar a sour look. Tamika laughed.

"Hey, Omar," she taunted, "what about the other day when *I* beat *you* at basketball? I thought you were gonna cry . . . boo-hoo, I got beat by a *girl*!"

Omar flushed angrily. "Okay, bighead! You were just lucky that time."

Tamika put her hands on her hips. "Hey! You stop calling me names, unless you wanna be popped!"

Raymond stepped between them. "Knock it off, Mika. Listen, this is Gordon, our new neighbor. He's nine, just like you."

"Almost ten," Gordon corrected.

Tamika looked him over. "Hi. You got any sisters?"

"Yeah, one. But she's sixteen."

"Oh." Tamika considered that, then shrugged. "Well, I'm glad you guys moved in instead of some grumpy old people."

Shuggie nodded wisely. "Like Mrs. Lewis?" The other kids laughed.

"Who's Mrs. Lewis?" Gordon asked.

"She's the lady who lives right across our alley," Raymond explained. "And since you're new, I'd better warn you—don't ever let a ball go over her fence! She's got this garden, and she gets mad if anybody steps in it. If our ball goes over her fence, we have to walk all the way around the block, ring her doorbell, and ask her to get it for us. Sometimes we just let her keep it and get a new one."

"And sometimes we sneak over her fence to get it ourselves," Shuggie said honestly.

Raymond frowned. "Unless you want to get yelled at, just stay away from Mrs. Lewis's garden. I don't think she likes kids."

The music began, "What child is this who laid to rest on Mary's breast is sleeping. . . . ?"

Raymond, listening through headphones, stared down at the church choir from his perch in the sound room. A solo was coming up, and he might need to adjust the microphone volume. He kept a close eye on his father, Raymond Brown, Senior. Mr. Brown would signal from his stool behind the drum set by holding up three or four fingers, then flashing a "thumbs up" or "thumbs down." That way Raymond would know which mike was being used, and whether to raise or lower the volume.

The job as sound man had been Raymond's for several years. He had first learned how to run the sound system when he was only ten years old. Now he attended choir rehearsal every Thursday night to get the equipment set up for Sunday morning. At age thirteen, he was in charge of both the sound system and the tape ministry.

The signal! Raymond quickly adjusted two of the knobs on the soundboard, then gave his dad a questioning look. Mr. Brown smiled and nodded, never missing a beat on his drums. Raymond relaxed again. Listening to the familiar Christmas carols made him wish Christmas would hurry up and get here.

Unless his parents ignored all the copies of his Christmas list that he'd "accidentally" left lying around, he should be getting a new basketball and hoop under the tree.

## A CRY FOR HELP

"Omar! Over here!"

Omar glanced at Gordon, but decided not to pass

the ball to him. Raymond was covering him, and even though it was Raymond's new Christmas basketball—and hoop, and yard—Omar didn't feel like letting him grab it.

As he hesitated, Shuggie rushed at him. Omar darted toward the goal, dribbled the ball twice, and took a shot. The ball sailed through the air and bounced off the rim.

"Man," Omar panted in disgust. His breath made cold puffs in the air as he bent over and propped his hands on his knees.

Gordon slapped him on the back. "Good try," he said kindly.

Raymond picked up the ball and tossed it from hand to hand, admiring it. It still smelled new. "You ready?" he asked.

Omar straightened and nodded. The game started again with lots of shouting.

They had a close call when Gordon took a shot that sent the ball flying into the alley by Mrs. Lewis's yard. Gordon sighed with relief when it bounced off the fence instead of landing in the garden. Since it was brand-new, he would've *had* to go ask Mrs. Lewis to get it.

Raymond dribbled the ball and darted past Omar. He was on the way up to try for a dunk when he heard a faint cry.

"Help! Somebody help me!"

Raymond faltered, missing the shot. When he hit the ground again, he stopped and looked around.

The other boys also froze, trying to figure out where the sound was coming from.

"Help! Please . . ."

Raymond frowned. His first thought was that it was just kids playing around. If so, he was going to yell at them. Saying "help!" should be saved for emergencies.

Then another voice, louder this time, shouted, "Somebody help my son!" This time, Raymond recognized the voice. It was Mrs. Lewis!

"Oh my gosh!" he shouted. "Something's wrong!" Dropping the basketball, Raymond sprinted for the stairs with Gordon, Omar, and Shuggie close behind. Raymond's family lived on the top floor, so the boys were out of breath by the time they burst in through the door.

"Mom!" shouted Raymond. "Quick, call 9-1-1!"

Mrs. Brown was in the middle of braiding Tamika's hair. She stopped, one half-done braid in her hand.

Tamika pulled away from her and jumped up, her hair sticking out in every direction. "What happened?"

"Mrs. Lewis is screaming for help!" Raymond said. "Just call 9-1-1!" He turned and ran back out the door, the other boys following.

Mrs. Brown grabbed the phone and started punching buttons. Tamika, seeing her chance, darted outside. She was only a few steps behind when the four boys pounded down the steps, across the yard, and into the back alley. They skidded to a stop outside Mrs. Lewis's fence.

Raymond looked across the fence into the backyard. At that angle he could see part of the driveway off on the other side, past the gate. Mr. and Mrs. Lewis were both out in the driveway, screaming and waving their arms.

Raymond vaulted over the fence.

After a moment's hesitation, the other four kids followed his lead. One by one, they scrambled over, landing in the middle of Mrs. Lewis's prized garden. The tomato plants got trampled underfoot as they raced across the yard and out through the gate.

At first glance, it was hard to tell what was wrong. A black Ford Fiesta was sitting on jacks in the driveway, with the front left wheel missing. As the kids spilled out into the driveway, Mrs. Lewis was desperately tugging at the front end of the car, trying to lift it.

"What's the matter?" Raymond asked, panting to a stop.

Mrs. Lewis was sobbing, her eyes wild with fear. "My son!" she gasped. "Help me get it off him!"

It was only then that the kids saw the man's brown hiking boots sticking out from under the side of the car.

## MISSION: IMPOSSIBLE

"Over here!" Mr. Lewis gasped. The elderly man was breathing from an oxygen tube in his nose, and each word took an effort. But as he waved frantically toward the front of the car, the kids realized what he wanted. They all rushed over to help Mrs. Lewis.

A quick glance at the man under the car left them terrified. When the jacks had slipped, the Ford had dropped, pinning Gary Lewis by his arm and chest beneath the heavy engine. He was gasping for air, unable to move. The 2,500-pound car threatened to crush him flat at any instant.

"Get it off me!" he begged in a gravelly whisper. His face was turned to one side to keep his head from being crushed.

Sobbing, Mrs. Lewis heaved at the front bumper again. "I can't get it, baby!" she cried.

Without thinking, the five kids lined up along the driver's side of the car. Raymond stood at the front, with Omar, Gordon, Shuggie, and Tamika lined up beside him. They each grabbed the part of the car in front of them and lifted with all their might.

The car barely inched upward.

Tamika's eyes grew wide. Within seconds, her small arms were shaking from the strain. To her horror, the car started to slip from her grasp.

"I'm dropping it!" she shrieked.

Omar, Shuggie, Gordon, and Raymond were all

having the same problem. One by one, they lost their grip. With a sickening *thump*, the car dropped back down on top of Gary Lewis.

There was a muffled gasp as the air was once again pushed from his lungs. Now he didn't even have enough breath to whisper. With the heavy engine pressing on his chest, he could only take short, panting breaths.

Raymond shouted excitedly, "Let's try it again! Everybody lift together on the count of three!"

Next to him, Omar bent his knees and curled his fingers around the opening on the front fender where the tire would usually be. On either side of him, Raymond and Gordon also got into position.

"One, two, *three*!"

Omar straightened his knees and heaved. The metal cut into his palms, and pain streaked up both his arms, but he didn't let go. Gordon, Shuggie, Tamika, and Raymond all did the same.

Once again, the front of the car edged upward.

On the concrete below, the unbearable pressure on Gary Lewis's chest suddenly let up. He sucked in a deep lungful of air with a noisy gasp. Then, terrified that the car would drop again, he dug in his heels and used his legs like a crab to pull himself forward.

Tamika stood with clenched teeth, arms trembling. She was squeezing the edge of the car so hard that her hands turned bright red. She squeezed even harder, determined not to let go this time.

It seemed to take forever for Gary to scoot clear of the car. Wheezing and coughing, he couldn't lift his head to see where he was going. He pulled himself forward blindly, praying that the thousands of pounds of metal wouldn't come crashing back down on him.

Tamika caught a glimpse of his face and shoulders when he finally slid out from under the driver's door. "He's out!" she yelled. The kids let go, sending the black car crashing to the ground.

Gary's face and lips were dark blue, and he was making a strange choking sound. "Air!" he croaked.

Mrs. Lewis dropped to her knees beside her son. "You're gonna be all right, baby," she said.

Shuggie gave Omar a scared look. The man didn't *look* like he was going to be all right. He looked almost dead. Shuggie had never seen a real person's face turn dark blue like that. He moved closer to his brother.

A siren wailed. "That's probably the ambulance," Raymond said. "My mom called 9-1-1 before we came over."

By the time the ambulance pulled into the driveway, Gary Lewis was sitting up. He still looked bad, but his face wasn't nearly as blue as it had been. He rubbed his chest and took deep breaths.

Before the ambulance took him away to the hospital, Gary pointed weakly to the five kids. "Those are my heroes,'' he told the rescue workers. ''They're my angels. They saved my life.''

As the kids turned to leave, Gordon noticed for the first time how badly they'd trampled the garden. After all the stories he'd heard about how much Mrs. Lewis loved it, he was afraid she'd be upset.

''I'm really sorry we stepped on your plants, Mrs. Lewis,'' he said. ''We didn't mean to.''

Mrs. Lewis wiped her eyes. ''Don't you worry about my garden, baby,'' she said. ''My son's life is worth more than a thousand gardens.''

## GOOD NEWS, BAD NEWS

The kids were surprised when a CNN News van pulled up in front of Raymond's house. People with TV cameras and microphones jumped out and ran over to them. Before they knew what was happening, they were shyly looking into the cameras and answering questions.

''Gary Lewis is alive and well, thanks to you five kids,'' the reporter said. ''What do you think made you able to lift a heavy car like that?''

''Angels helped us,'' said Tamika. ''Well, and I eat a lot of cheese.'' The reporter laughed.

It wasn't until they saw themselves on TV, though, that Omar, Shuggie, Gordon, Raymond, and Tamika learned that they were being called ''The

Rescue Team.'' It made them all giggle. They were heroes!

Not everything that happened afterward was funny, though. Several days after the rescue, Mrs. Turner got a phone call that left her speechless. She slammed down the phone and turned to Omar and Shuggie, her face flushed and angry.

''I don't believe this!'' she said. ''The company that's been paying your doctor bills saw you two on the news. They said that if you can go around picking up cars, you don't need any more physical therapy! What were you two *thinking* to do such a thing?''

Omar sputtered, ''But Mom, that's not right! What did you want us to do, stand there and tell that guy, 'Sorry, we're not allowed to lift, so you're just going to have to die'?''

Mrs. Turner stared at him, then at Shuggie. Slowly, the angry lines on her face softened.

''No,'' she said, ''that's not what I would've wanted. You did the right thing and no matter what happens, I'll always be proud of you for that.''

*Gary Lewis recovered completely, except for a small scar on his right shoulder. The National Dairy Council sent Tamika, Shuggie, Omar, Gordon, and Raymond ''Got Milk?'' hats and several cases of cheese.*

ABOVE: Tamika and Shuggie.

LEFT: "The Rescue Team."

Kids! Have you heard or read about someone who should be a "Real Kid"? We're always looking for new stories for future volumes of *Real Kids, Real Adventures*—true stories about young survivors and heroes. If you've heard about a story that might work, send a newspaper clipping or other information to:

> REAL KIDS, REAL ADVENTURES
> STORY TIPS
> P.O. BOX 461572
> GARLAND, TEXAS 75046-1572

You can also E-mail us at: *storytips@realkids.com*. Remember to include your name and phone number in case we need to contact you.

If your story is chosen for use in a future volume of *Real Kids, Real Adventures* (and you were the first one to send that particular story in), you will receive a free, autographed copy of the book and have your name mentioned at the end of the story.

Visit the Real Kids Real Adventures™ official website at:

> http://www.realkids.com

The *Real Kids, Real Adventures* book series is now a hit TV series!

Meet the "Real Kids" every Sunday morning at 10:30 A.M. ET/PT (9:30 A.M. Central) on the Discovery Channel. Each exciting half-hour episode shows the true story of a young hero or survivor— and at the end of each show, you'll meet the *real* "Real Kid" from that week's story.

The ADVENTURE starts here. Don't miss it!

# ABOUT THE AUTHOR

Deborah Morris, one of the nation's leading writers of real-life dramas, has authored twelve books and over one hundred magazine articles featured in *Reader's Digest, Family Circle*, and *Good Housekeeping*. She has also co-produced two TV movies, and is creator/co-producer of the *Real Kids, Real Adventures* TV series based on her books.

Deborah lives in Garland, Texas, and can be reached by E-mail at *deb@realkids.com*.